Jan Kjær & Merlin P. Mann

TAYNIKMA

Book 4: The Lost Catacombs

D1322435

Young World Digital
MMIX

TAYNIKMA
Book 4: The Lost Catacombs
(Original title: De Glemte Katakomber)

Translated by Kathryn Mahaffy

© Jan Kjær & Merlin P. Mann
© This edition Young World Digital Ltd, London, U.K.

ISBN 978-0-9558337-3-1
First edition

Published by:
Young World Digital Ltd • PO Box 6268 • London W1A 2HE
www.youngworlddigital.com

Printed and bound in Great Britain in 2009
by Stanley L. Hunt (Printers) Ltd, Rushden, Northants

All rights reserved. No part of this publication may be reproduced, stored in a
retrieval system, or transmitted in any form or by any means, electronic, mechanical,
photo-copying, recording or otherwise, without the prior permission of the publishers.

British Library Cataloguing in Publication Data available.

TAYNIKMA
Book 1: Master Thief
Book 2: The Rats
Book 3: Tower of the Sun
Book 4: The Lost Catacombs
Book 5: The Secret Arena
Book 6: Duel of the Clans
Book 7: Henzel's Ambush
Book 8: The Forest of Shadows
Book 9: The Fortress of Light
Book 10: The Final Battle

www.taynikma.co.uk

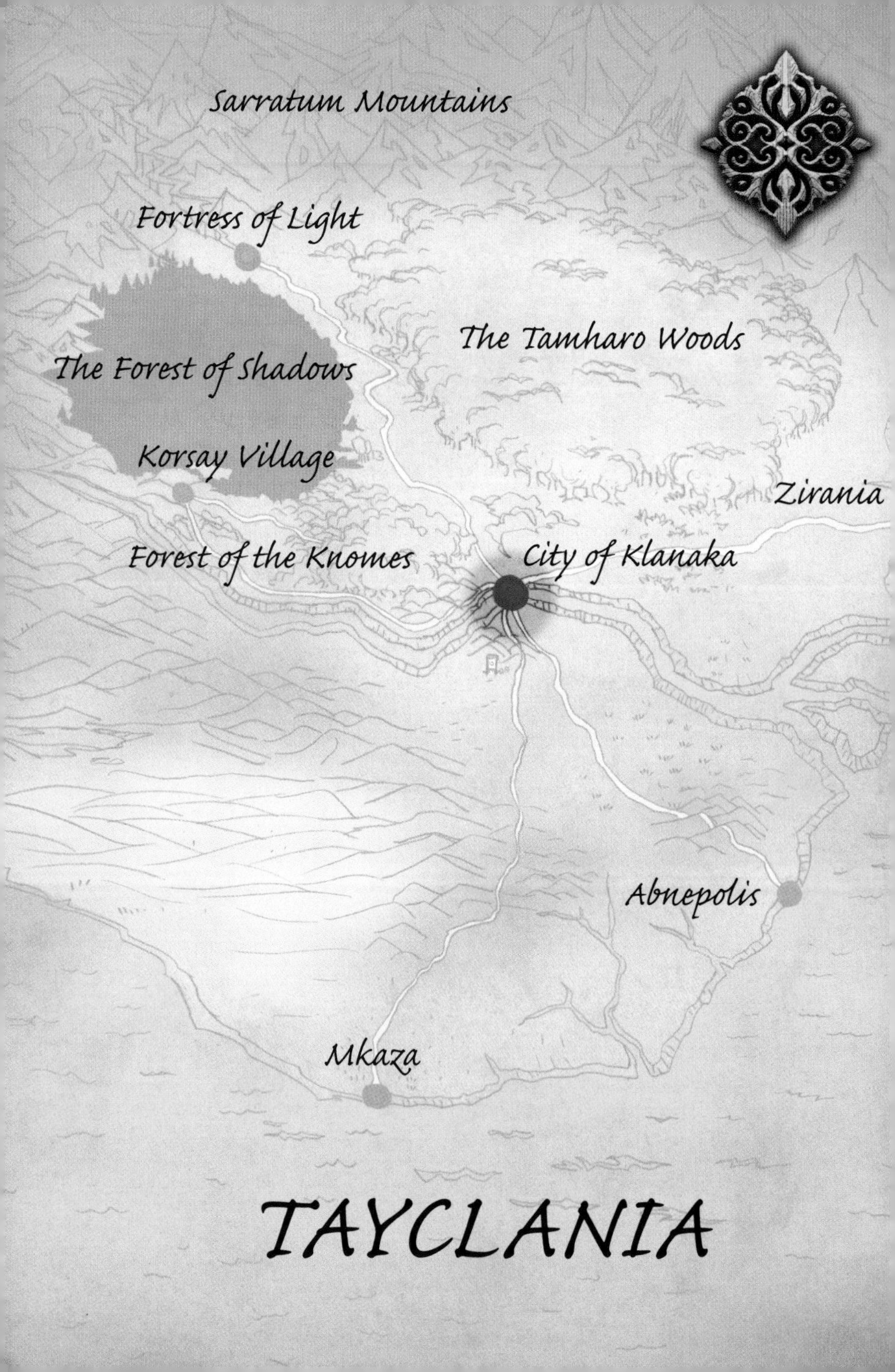

Sarratum Mountains

Fortress of Light

The Tamharo Woods

The Forest of Shadows

Korsay Village

Zirania

Forest of the Knomes

City of Klanaka

Abnepolis

Mkaza

TAYCLANIA

Tayclania

South of the mountains, north of the sea lies the land of Tayclania.

For hundreds of years it was a haven for merchants, craftsmen and scholars. The land was ruled by the four clans: The Sun, The Moon, The Mountain and The River.

Each clan had its deities and powers. The Sun Clan had the healing powers of light, the Moon Clan had the protection of shadow, the Mountain Clan had raw strength and the River Clan had wisdom.

Even though it was a land of plenty, quarrels began between the clans. Quarrels led to fights.
Fights led to war.

A treaty was signed, but few believed the four clans could rule together again.

Peace was short-lived. A sorceress murdered three champions from each clan and from their souls she created a total of 12 invincible knights: the Sentinels. Soon all of Tayclania had to bow to her rule and she became The Empress.

The clans were outlawed, the borders were closed and The Empress imposed the Law of the Sun. She declared that only by having just one deity could the land live in peace and harmony. A brief uprising was attempted by the clans but easily crushed by the Sentinels.

Soon the rule of the immortal Empress of Light will have lasted for 100 years.

ARTAN

13 years old and wise beyond his years. He was accepted to the River Clan Academy even though he is an orphan. A strong-willed dreamer.

KERN

Artan's worst rival at the River Clan Academy. He comes from a posh clan family and would like to see Artan thrown out. Feared by the other apprentices.

KOTO

14 years old and Master Thief Gekko's apprentice. He has supernatural gifts in taming shadows and possesses a magic taynikma. He is seeking to make a living for his family, but is always ready to help others.

MONTO

16 years old and a member of the Mountain Clan. Was meant to follow his deceased father as a soldier but is now fighting to overthrow the evil Captain Henzel. Monto's taynikma gets its power from the rocks and mountains.

The story so far ...

Koto and his parents need money before winter, and Koto has gone to the city Klanaka to seek it. There he becomes apprenticed to the master thief Gekko and Koto discovers his special shadow powers.

... your dad will never have to worry about Lord Tuskan again!

After a perilous adventure he has regained his magic taynikma. Master Gekko has sent him out to make contact with the outlawed clans, who are struggling against the evil rule of Captain Henzel.

WHOA!?

TENE-FALANX!

On his travels Koto meets the soldier Monto. He is searching for his uncle, who turns out to be an agent for the Mountain Clan. Koto and Monto rescue him from Henzel's horrible prison, The Tower of the Sun.

They are weak without the sunlight! Get them!

The Mountain Taynikma!

Together they return to the secret city of the Clans, and Monto is proclaimed a warrior of the Mountain Clan.

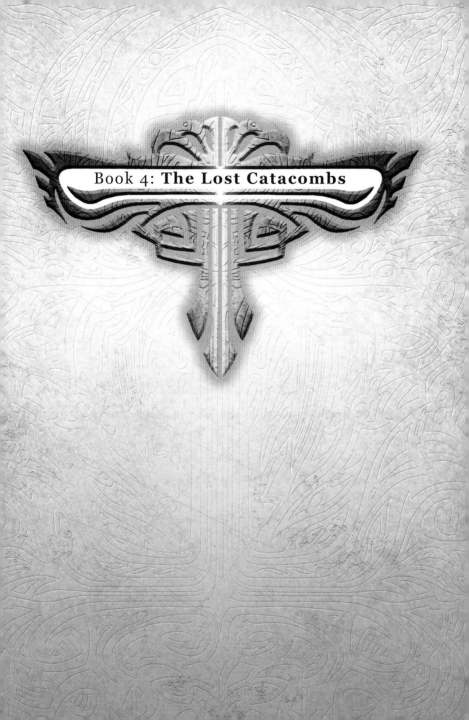

Book 4: **The Lost Catacombs**

The Labyrinth

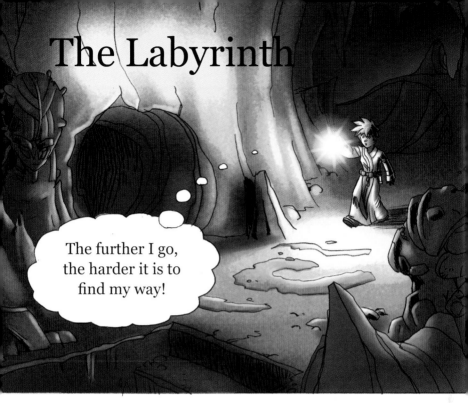

The further I go, the harder it is to find my way!

Artan had been wandering through narrow, crumbling tunnels for hours. Though he had been trying hard to remember the way, he was starting to despair – Where was he? He set his lantern down and wiped the sweat from his brow.

»It was a perfect plan. I would have been through the labyrinth by now if that blasted portal hadn't been impossible to open!«

All at once Artan heard a distant scratching noise. He had heard it several times before on his quest. Artan swallowed hard.

I wonder what that could be?

It was nothing nice, that was pretty certain. Another good reason to find the right way out in a hurry! He picked up the lantern and went on.

»Right or left?« muttered Artan, as he arrived at a branching passage. »I've got to get out of here before I really lose my way ...« Artan stepped into the cross-tunnel. He squatted down and raised the glass lantern-chimney. The flame flickered, and Artan smiled.

An air current from the right!

There must be a way out there!

Artan lowered the lantern's glass and stepped boldly down the right-hand tunnel.

»The floor may give way at any minute,« thought Artan, shuddering. »I've got to get out of here as fast as I can.«

Artan's heart was hammering and his breath came short. Luckily he glimpsed a sliver of light at the end of the tunnel. Through a narrow crevice Artan could see light but as he squeezed through the lantern caught on the edge of the opening and fell out of his hand.

»Why does everything go wrong for me?!« shouted Artan, emerging on the other side. He kicked the rock wall in a fit of temper.

Artan was just about to squeeze back through the crevice when a big fist grabbed his collar. »Take it easy! We're not going to hurt you!« said a voice.

Artan turned around. All of a sudden he saw that he was in an enormous cave. He had lived in Netherville all his life but he didn't know this part of it. Each clan had its own territory in Netherville, and Artan had only lived in the River Clan quarter. The clans had no dealings with each other.

Who are you?

My name's Monto!

And that's Koto!

»How did you end up here underground where the Mountain Clan live?« asked Koto, brushing the worst of the dust off Artan's shoulder.

»M-mountain Clan! But ... they're wild barbarians!« stammered Artan, cringing back. »Don't hit me!«

Monto and Koto looked at each other. Then they started to laugh. »Why in the world should we hit you?« said Koto. »We don't even know who you are.«

I'm Artan. Apprentice to the River Clan Academy.

»The River Clan?« exclaimed Monto. »What the blazes are you doing here, then?«

Artan sighed. »That's a good question …« He looked at Koto and Monto. They didn't look like the sort who would attack him. Artan smiled and breathed easier. He wasn't in any danger – for the moment, at least.

»It's on account of the Crystal Challenge. You see, the River Clan Academy holds a kind of contest. All the apprentices compete for the title of First Apprentice – the highest honour you can gain! And I was sure I could win …«

Reading-Master Lorgo explained the rules to us a few days ago.

Only the most learned apprentice can win the Crystal Challenge!

»My worst rival was Kern. He's always hated me.«

Not only must he find his way through the labyrinth to the Crystal Cave ...

»Lorgo went on: "He must also solve all the tasks along the way. These must be met with craft, cunning and wisdom – and mistakes will spring traps to hinder the apprentice's forward path! Should he reach the Crystal Cave, he must take one of the rare blue crystals. The first apprentice who, by his own skill – without help of any kind – can bring a blue crystal back to the Council, will be proclaimed the River Clan's First Apprentice!"«

I've always wanted to be First Apprentice ...

»And it's not the labyrinth or the tasks I'm afraid of. Not at all. I knew exactly which books to read so I could solve the riddles and find my way through the labyrinth. It's Kern – it's him I'm scared of. He said he would kill me!«

»The evening before the start of the Crystal Challenge, Kern caught me down in the library. "Give me your notes, Artan!" he hissed, after he was sure we were alone.«

Yell for help and I'll rip your tongue out!

»When Kern says something like that, you believe him. It didn't really matter about the notes, because I had them all in my head – and I was still sure I could be the first to get through the labyrinth.«

»But then he said: ...« Artan sighed and drew a deep breath.

If you show up for the Crystal Challenge, I'll kill you as soon as we're in the labyrinth!

»I knew that as soon as we got in there no one would see what happened.«

»"Someone always gets badly hurt during the Crystal Challenge", Kern said with an evil laugh. "If I were you, I'd stay in bed tomorrow!"«

Koto and Monto had been listening attentively to Artan's tale and as soon as Artan fell silent, Koto burst out: »Go on! What did you do then?«

»Kern can threaten to kill me, he can steal my notes,« said Artan with a wry smile, »But he'll never be as smart as I am! While I was preparing myself to walk the labyrinth, I found an ancient manuscript that told of other tunnels that also might lead to the Crystal Cave. No one knew of those old tunnels now but I found a hidden entrance. So instead of showing up for the Crystal Challenge at the entrance of the labyrinth, I just slipped around and took a shortcut. And I would be standing in the Crystal Cave this minute – if the entrance back into the labyrinth hadn't been locked!«

It's no use! It won't open!

»I've been wandering these passages for hours looking for another way out. And now I'm here ...«

All is lost!

Artan slumped down onto the floor of the cave with a deep sigh. He sat staring blankly at nothing. Koto and Monto shared a resolute glance. »Oh no, it's not!« said Koto, while Monto pulled Artan onto his feet. »I just happen to be the world's champion picklock ...«

And Monto is the world's champion at giving bullies like Kern their comeuppance!

»We were on our way up to Koto's master but we'd be glad to give you a hand first!« smiled Monto.

Artan gazed at the two boys in amazement. »Would you really? But I've heard that people from the other clans are a lot of savage barbarians,« said Artan.

»And I've heard that everyone in the River Clan is a stuck-up sissy,« laughed Monto. »But that's not so, is it?«

Artan smiled and shook his head but then turned serious again: »I smashed my lamp ...«

»Never mind! I have a good torch,« smiled Monto.

»There's the portal,« said Artan, pointing. It was hard to see because it was flush with the rock wall. It had been closed for many years. Koto found the lock, feeling with his fingers. Then he began to mumble strange words.

Is that a ... taynikma?

That's right!

How did you know that?

I've read a lot about the Taytans and their nikmas.

I just didn't think they existed anymore.

Koto smiled, as the lock opened with a click. »Well, luckily, they do!« With a cheerful look he tried to push open the massive portal – but in vain!

»It just sticks a bit,« said Monto. »Let me have a go. I've got a taynikma, too – and mine is from the Mountain Clan!«

Monto laid his hand on the portal, and at once his arm began to draw magic power from the mountains. The taynikma gave him super-human strength!

TERA-BOTAN!

A colossal cloud of dust flew up, making the three boys cough.

»Couldn't you just have opened it?" asked Koto, wiping dust out of his eyes.«

»Sorry,« mumbled Monto. »I'm not quite used to it yet …«

Artan wasted no time. »Come on!« he whispered, running through the shattered portal. »We've got to find the Crystal Cave before …« Artan stopped short in the labyrinth passage.

Before …?

»You!?« cried Kern. »Didn't I tell you to stay at home, you little worm?«

Kern narrowed his eyes. »Well, well – so the little brat brought along some big boys to play with,« he spat out. »That's against the rules, Artan. You're a cheat!«

»So are you!« shouted Artan, stepping defiantly toward Kern. »You stole my notes – and you threatened to kill me. But now you'll get what's coming to you!«

Monto and Koto exchanged a smile and walked steadily toward Kern. The beefy boy looked hastily around him, then yanked one of three levers that stuck out of the wall and bolted off down the passage.

Koto and Monto jumped back just in time as the metal grating crashed down in front of them. They were unharmed – but trapped!

You've got yourself some pretty useless pals there, Artan!

»If you get a task wrong, the trap is sprung. Now you fools can just sit there and chat while I go find the crystal!«

»He mustn't get away,« gasped Artan, as Kern quickly moved out of sight.

»Don't worry,« growled Monto. »I'll soon move this rusty junk.«

Monto summoned all his strength and pushed hard at the heavy grating. At first it didn't budge, then the ancient metal started to groan.

»You've almost got it, Monto,« said Koto, clapping him on the back. »Your taynikma just needs to draw more strength from the rocks. You can do it!«

»T-tera-bo-tan!« panted Monto who was sweating heavily by now. The taynikma on his wrist began to flicker – and at last something gave way ...

It's falling
back this way!

Their eyes flew to the creaking grating that was about
to plummet toward them.

»Whoops!« said Monto, and took to his heels. The
grating crashed to the ground and the cracks it made in
the stone were widening much too quickly. In a flash the
cracks had become a chasm.

Your taynikma
weakened the
rock, Monto!

Koto, Monto and Artan looked at the deep, wide hole.
There was no way over. Artan wormed his way to the edge
and peered down.

Th-there's
something
down there ...

The Lost Catacombs

Could it be true? Artan had read in some of the old writings of ancient caves and halls that were said to lie even deeper than Netherville, but no one could say whether the tales were true. Reading-Master Lorgo had only told him that heroes and kings were long ago buried in tombs deep underground. But now none dared to seek a way down there. Down to ...

»Cata-what?« demanded Monto, who had arrived at the edge of the pit.

»The taytans were buried here,« Artan told him. »No one can have been down there for a hundred years and more. No one knows what may be hidden in the Lost Catacombs. We must get down there right away!«

Koto smiled wryly at Artan, who seemed to have forgotten all about his quest.

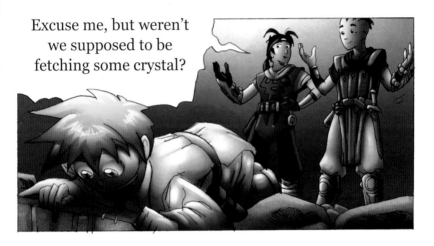

Excuse me, but weren't we supposed to be fetching some crystal?

Artan looked at him, then his eyes wandered dazedly around the stone passage. »Er – yes, of course,« he said, scratching his neck. »But we can't get over this pit. Maybe we can find a shortcut that goes UNDER the labyrinth!«

Koto and Monto exchanged glances. There was some sense in Artan's idea. »Tene-Gara!« said Koto, and drew a sturdy rope out of the shadows; they shinned down it into the great, dark hall.

»That must be one of the holy stones,« said Artan cautiously stepping toward a large stone table. He could almost hear Lorgo's voice as he slowly deciphered the finely carved inscriptions. »This was where they performed sacred rituals for the fallen taytans.«

»Why are there symbols here from other clans?« Monto asked. »This is River Clan territory, isn't it?«

»In the old days the clans worked together,« said Artan. »The River Clan had charge of burying the heroes, no matter which clan they belonged to.«

Artan had dreamt about the age of the taytans for years, and now he stood in the midst of legends.

The fallen heroes were preserved as mummies.

Their bodies last for thousands of years!

»You two might enjoy chatting about mummies,« said Koto uneasily, »But don't you think we'd better hurry? I think I'd like to –«

What was that noise?

Koto and Artan held their breath and listened intently. At first Artan heard nothing but then the sound of scraping began again. »I've heard that sound before,« said Artan with a shudder. »But it's coming closer now!«

»Then let's be on our way,« said Koto, striding rapidly toward one of the many vaulted arches that all led into murky passages. There was an inscription over the archway.

»*You can take the path only once,*« read Artan. »Wait!« he cried, but Koto and Monto were already on their way down the passage.

»Blast! Dead end!« said Koto, when they had gone a little way. He took one more step, and all at once there was a click from the floor. The ground trembled, and the walls began to move with a deep rumbling sound.

»What's going on?« shouted Monto. A cloud of dust billowed up as the passage closed behind them – while the wall in front of them slid aside, revealing a new passage.

The walls can move!

The catacombs are a labyrinth that changes as you move through it.

»That's not fair!« said Koto, kicking up the dust. »That means we'll never get out of here!«

Artan went past Koto and peered into the passage that ran at right angles to the one they were in. He shut his eyes tight and tried to recall what Reading-Master Lorgo had told them about the Lost Catacombs. "Only destiny can show the way," he had said. »We'll just have to see what happens,« said Artan, and went ahead.

He might look like a wimp ...

But he's no coward!

»Neither am I!« snapped Koto as they followed Artan.
»I'm just not all that crazy about burial vaults. It might
be dangerous to disturb graARRH!« Koto tripped over
something on the tunnel floor, and Artan and Monto
hurried to help him to his feet.

»It's a skeleton ... « Koto shuddered. »I guess others
before us have tried to get through the catacombs. And
didn't make it!«

Artan stared at the bones. There was something
uncanny about them.

»Monto – bring the light over here!« Artan bent over
the skeleton. »Look at those claws,« he whispered.

Whatever it is, it isn't human ...

»I don't care what it is,« said Koto, »as long as it stays where it is! Can we get on now?«

Koto turned to go, but before he had taken three steps the earth started to tremble again. The walls rumbled, and the labyrinth had changed again.

Koto's right!

We don't have time to study bones. We've got to get out before the labyrinth locks us in!

Artan looked up and caught sight of a doorway that had just appeared. Above it, in ornate script, was engraved: »The Remembrancer«. Artan walked closer.

»Are you sure we should go that way?« asked Koto uneasily. Artan shook his head.

»You can't be sure of anything here,« said Artan.

But it's as if destiny is pulling me in here …

Artan gasped. Never had he seen anything like this. Koto and Monto followed him cautiously along rows of old writing desks and stacks of paper.

What's this thing?

»It must be an ancient machine,« Said Artan, going closer to it. »It's made up of lots of small nikmas!«

He laid his hand carefully on the figure ... and the mechanical eyes opened with a metallic shriek.

»In life we are silent. In death we lament below your feet! Who are we?« creaked a voice from the machine.

Koto and Monto fell back with a cry and drew their taynikmas, ready to do battle.

Stop!

I don't think it means us harm!

Artan was staring at the strange face of the figure.

»In life we are silent. In death we lament below your feet! Who are we?« repeated the mask-like head in its mechanical voice.

»It's a riddle!« Artan smiled.

Typical of the River Clan, using riddles as the key to their nikmas. You know the answer, don't you?

Artan didn't wait for a reply. »The leaves of a tree! Alive the leaves are silent, but the dead, fallen ones rustle underfoot!«

»That is correct,« said the thing. »I am the Remembrancer. At your service, young master ...«

Artan blushed and smiled bashfully. »I'm not a master ... yet. But if I can find the Crystal Cave quickly, I can be First Apprentice!«

The neck of the Remembrancer creaked as it peered up searchingly at Artan. »Hmmm ...« it buzzed, and laid its hand carefully on his shoulder. »It is not the Crystal Cave you seek,« it said after a long silence. Artan stared in amazement at the automaton. Koto and Monto moved nearer.

»Er – well, actually it is,« said Artan. »Can you help me?«

The Remembrancer nodded. »You shall be guided on the right way!« it said.

»Will you lead me to the Crystal Cave?« asked Artan hopefully.

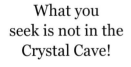

What you seek is not in the Crystal Cave!

You have a vital task to do. That is why you have come to the Remembrancer ...

»But – my task is to find the Crystal Cave!« said Artan, throwing his arms wide. »I have to bring back a blue crystal!« The Remembrancer seemed to pay no heed. The many small nikmas in its body began to whirr and buzz. It sounded almost as if the Remembrancer took a deep breath before it spoke again:

Although the clans lost the first battle of Tayclania many years ago, the war is not yet over. Since the Empress defeated the taytans, she has kept herself alive by magic arts.

But she is not invincible ...

Not yet!

»For many long years she has striven to reach her final goal: to merge herself with the Sun's power and become a goddess. A *remorseless* goddess that none can resist!«

Koto, Monto and Artan listened carefully. Artan knew the story of the Empress – the enchantress who vanquished the clans. But she had not been seen for countless years, and many thought that she was only a myth. Now everyone feared Henzel and his soldiers.

»Her servants have put down all resistance with every means at their command, and soon the last remnants of the clans will be wiped out. Then none will be able to stop the Empress from becoming invincible.«

Except for The One Taytan!

A taytan? But – they're all dead!

I don't know when you last heard news from the world outside, but there are no heroes left ...

For the first time since it began its long speech, the Remembrancer paused and looked at Artan, Monto and Koto. »A new one will come,« it said. »With your help.«

Us?

What are we supposed to do?

»Find the River taynikma,« said the Remembrancer.

Artan's jaw dropped. The River taynikma? What wouldn't he give to see it!

»What do we want with a River taynikma?« asked Monto sceptically.

»The River taynikma must call the clans to a gathering, so that they may find The One Taytan.«

Just a minute!

We have no time for that! For one thing, we have to get out of here, and for another, Artan has to win that Crystal Challenge thing!

Besides, we have no idea where the River taynikma might be ...

The Remembrancer pointed at the wall, where a long bookcase began to slide slowly to one side. Behind it, a narrow flight of stairs led down into the darkness.

»Down there!« said the Remembrancer. »Seek the symbol of The One Taytan. But be careful. The diggers are drawing closer than ever ...«

The Diggers

»I don't know how you dragged us into all this, Artan,«
said Koto with a nervous smile, as they went cautiously
down to the nethermost burial chamber. Artan swallowed
hard. He didn't know how he'd gotten into it himself.

»Do you know who "the diggers" are?« asked Monto.
Artan could only shake his head.

They reached the foot of the stairs, and even with the
help of Monto's light it was hard to see anything. The
room seemed to be nothing but an ancient cave, but in
the middle of it was a big, dark sarcophagus. On the lid
was a mysterious four-part symbol.

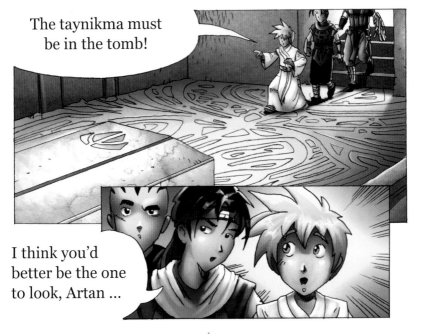

The taynikma must
be in the tomb!

I think you'd
better be the one
to look, Artan ...

Artan was trembling from head to foot, and he felt as though he was in the kind of nightmare where you can't move or scream. He took a deep breath and went up to the sarcophagus. With Monto's help he managed to push the lid aside, revealing a ghastly mummy.
And there it lay ...

The River taynikma!

Isn't this robbing a grave?

No! It was just hidden away here ...

»Besides, it was our destiny to find it!« said Artan, trying to appear calm.

»But won't the sky fall on our heads if you take it?« asked Koto nervously.

»Of course not,« said Artan, lifting the taynikma out carefully, »That's just an old superstition ...«

CRRRRACK! Suddenly a long sinister-looking crevice appeared in the ceiling over the staircase.

»It is falling on our heads!« gasped Koto in panic, as the crack widened into a gaping hole.

»No« said Monto. »But someone's on the way out of that hole! Quick ... we've got to get out of here!«

They dashed back toward the stairs, but it was too late!

Those must be the diggers!

»Now for it, Koto!« roared Monto. »Tene-sora!« cried Koto, and the battle was on!

TERA-GORKO!

Terrified, Artan threw himself down behind a rock, while Koto and Monto used their powers against the diggers.

»If it is my destiny to find the taynikma,« Artan wailed, »why am I losing it now?«

»You're not going to lose anything!« said Monto breathlessly. »We'll keep them at bay. Come on!«

Koto managed to keep the diggers off just long enough for the boys to get back up the stairs. They quickly dragged the heavy bookcase back in place.

It won't be long before they've hacked their way through!

Monto ran to the Remembrancer, but the automaton had slumped forward, looking almost as if it had dozed off.

»Hey! Remembrancer!« shouted Monto, shaking the metal form. »We found that taynikma, and now you've got to help us out of here in a hurry! Wake up!«

The Remembrancer opened its eyes slowly. »I run and stand still – always on my way, always in the same place. Shaped like a snake, but not poisonous. Who am I?«

Another riddle?
NOT NOW!

You miserable
pile of scrap!

Tell us the way out!

But the Remembrancer just repeated its riddle. Artan ran to it, while Koto and Monto tried feverishly to block the stairs with desks, chairs and more bookcases.

Runs and
stands still.
Snake, but not
poisonous …

Normally Artan would have solved the riddle as quick as blinking, but it wasn't so easy to think straight with slavering subterranean monsters hacking their way in …

No more
River riddles
now!

Let's be on our
way, Artan!

River? At last! The answer to the riddle.

»You both run and stand still. Always on your way, always in the same place. Shaped like a snake, but not poisonous. You are the river!«

»Correct!« creaked the Remembrancer, as Koto and Monto stared dumbfounded at little, clever Artan.

All right!
Now tell us the
way out.

He will
show the
way ...

Artan shook his head in bewilderment. »What? But you've got to help us! I solved the riddle, and ...« Artan got no further; with a tremendous crash the bookcase in front of stairway gave way, and the diggers crowded into the chamber. They hacked down the barricade of furniture that Monto and Koto had heaped up.

»We have to get out!« shouted Monto. »Never mind it, Artan. Run!« Koto and Monto bolted for the doorway, but Artan grabbed the Remembrancer's metal arm.

»Oh, please help me, Remembrancer!« Artan pleaded fervently, trying to catch the eye of the mystic machine. »Tell us the way!«

»The labyrinth is constantly shifting. The way cannot be told,« said the Remembrancer. »You must find it yourself, with the help of ...« At that instant one of the diggers sprang like a tiger on the Remembrancer.

It dug its claw into the head of the machine with a mighty crunch. Wild sparks and lightning flew to right and left.

»Tay ... nikma!« sighed the Remembrancer, before it slumped to the floor for the last time.

»Taynikma? What did it mean by that?« muttered Artan, gingerly fingering the precious object he was clutching in his arms.

»Look out, Artan!« roared Monto, as the digger leapt again. »Tene-sora!« shouted Koto, and beat the creature off with his shadow-whip just in the nick of time. Artan almost dropped the taynikma as he stumbled towards Koto and Monto.

Move!
Come on!

But I'll
drop the
taynikma!

»Well, put it on then!« said Koto. »Hurry up! I can't keep them off much longer!«

Artan threw himself behind Koto. He looked at the taynikma, panting. At that moment it opened with a loud click!

Put it on ...?

Artan swallowed hard and laid his arm inside the taynikma. SWACK! It snapped shut around Artan's wrist as if it were moulded to his forearm.

»It suits you, Artan,« said Koto. »Now let's get out of here!«

But the doorway was shut. Once more The Labyrinth had shifted; a wall had shoved its way in front of the entrance.

What the blazes ...?!

»It's all over!« With shaking hands, Artan hammered on the wall that blocked their flight.

A huge spark flashed from Artan's taynikma as he touched the wall. It began to glow and a curious pulse of sound came from it. The earth began to rumble, and the three boys looked at each other.

»Let's hope you just got the labyrinth to change back,« said Koto.

Because otherwise things look bad for us.

»The wall is moving!« Monto shouted gladly. They dashed through the doorway. The diggers hissed and rushed after them. Koto and Monto sprinted ahead, but suddenly Artan stopped and stared at his taynikma. Something was beginning to appear in the air above it. Glowing letters.

»It's a word,« said Artan, and held up his arm in front of the doorway. At that moment the diggers reached the portal and the foremost one was heading for Artan.

ARKI-MORU!

»That's what I call slamming the door.« Koto grinned at Artan, who was standing there gasping for breath. He had saved them – with his taynikma!

»I'm afraid we can't stand around and celebrate,« said Monto, clapping Artan and Koto on the back. »There's still a mob of vermin in there, and who knows when they'll be able to dig their way in.«

»But we still don't know which way to go!« said Koto, flinging out his arms. Artan stood still, studying the taynikma.

Look here!

That was what the Remembrancer meant! The taynikma can show us the way!

Smiling eagerly, Artan set off running back and forth down the passage, and as he moved, the images the taynikma revealed changed, so new passages and openings kept coming in view.

»I hope it's the way out it's showing us,« murmured Monto, as he and Koto followed Artan at a run.

The Crystal Challenge

Though his cloak wasn't made for running in, Artan was setting a good pace now. He shouted and sang as the taynikma led him through the Lost Catacombs. Koto and Monto couldn't help smiling as they tried their best to keep up.

There's a stairway leading up!

Koto and Monto stood behind him, panting.

»It didn't take you long to learn how to use your taynikma« grinned Koto. Artan nodded.

»It's as if it's been lying there waiting for me,« he said with a shy smile.

»You'll have to wait till later for your little chat,« Monto grumbled. »We're not out yet!«

»I know what you mean,« whispered Koto, winking at Artan, as they all started to climb the stairs.

»Blast! It's a dead end!« growled Monto.

»Don't let it fool you,« said Artan, reading his floating air-map.

There's a cave on the other side …

And unless I'm much mistaken, it's the Crystal Cave.

»Well, let's get on with it, then,« said Monto, taking a deep breath. He was just about to use his taynikma to knock a whole in the wall, when Artan threw himself in front of him.

»Stop! The Cave is full of crystals. You could smash the lot! You'd better let me …«

Monto glared indignantly at Artan. Then he folded his arms and stalked over to Koto. »You'd think I go around smashing everything in sight,« he muttered sulkily.

»Watch!« said Artan, waving his right arm in front of the wall. »I can feel something happening in the taynikma!«

Artan laid his hand on the wall, and the taynikma began to glow.

The secret door slid open almost without a sound. A bright light, every colour of the rainbow, shone from the opening.

»Leaping landslides!« gasped Koto, throwing up his hands in front of his face. Artan and Monto also had to shield their eyes as they peered in.

I was right!

»There are millions of crystals,« Koto said.

»Yes, but we just need one of the blue ones,« said Artan, and with Monto's help he chipped off a beautiful bluish crystal.

Artan's eyes filled with happy tears. At last! There he stood with the crystal in his hands.

I don't know how I can ever thank you!

»Don't mention it,« said Koto. »Monto and I know what it's like to need a helping hand!«

»Hadn't you better hurry up and deliver that crystal now?« asked Monto. »Who knows, that Kern character might have been here already, while we were messing about down in the catacombs.«

Artan and Koto nodded. The important thing now was get back to the academy as fast as they could. And luckily Artan's taynikma could show them the quickest way out.

»Do you want us to come in with you?« asked Koto, when they got to the main door of the Academy. Artan blushed painfully. He was supposed to have found the crystal by himself.

»You mustn't be seen,« Artan whispered, »or they'll know I cheated!«

»Cheated? What do you mean?« asked Monto.

Kern was right when he called me a cheat!

You're supposed to find the crystal on your own.

Without help from anyone else ...

»That's just stupid!« said Koto. »But don't worry – we won't snitch. We'll hide outside«

Hesitantly, Artan pushed open the door to the great entry hall. In the opposite wall another door stood ajar. It was there Reading-Master Lorgo sat waiting. Artan took a deep breath and walked toward the room, hugging the blue crystal to his chest.

»Stop!« hissed a well-known voice behind him. Artan turned with a startled croak as Kern stepped out of the shadows. »I don't know how you and your lousy pals got out of the trap, but it's lucky for me you did!«

»Wh-what do you mean?« stammered Artan.

»I saw you in the labyrinth,« said Kern, taking a step nearer. »At the rate you were going, I could tell you must have found something. I followed you, and while you were standing at the front door, I slipped in through the back way!« Kern was only a step away from Artan now. A crafty smile spread over his face.

I'll take that!

»NO! I'm the one who found it!« cried Artan, snatching the crystal out of Kern's hands.

»You cheated, you worm,« said Kern, grabbing Artan by the collar. »Give me that, if you want to keep your front teeth!«

I'm not scared of you anymore!

I've taken care of worse monsters than you!

Kern stared at Artan in surprise. Then he drove his fist into the smaller boy's stomach. Artan doubled up, dropping the crystal on the floor.

What is going
on here?

Reading-Master Lorgo came toward the two boys.

Kern hurriedly picked up the crystal and drew back a step.

»Artan cheated!« said Kern, pointing at Artan, who had not yet recovered from the blow. »He got two big boys to help him in the labyrinth. They're hiding outside. I saw it myself!«

The Reading Master walked right up to the boys. He looked long and searchingly at both Kern and Artan.

»Is this true?« asked Lorgo, taking Artan's arm to help him to his feet.

Artan finally caught his breath and was about to speak, but Lorgo took a firmer grip on his arm, and stared directly into his eyes.

You know you
cannot lie to your
master!

Artan swallowed hard. »Yes ... but Kern didn't find the crystal ...« said Artan. Lorgo silenced him, laying a finger on his lips.

»His stupid friends threatened me!« Kern said.

I could have found the cave, but they were going to beat me up!

Artan was about to protest, but Lorgo just nodded.

But —

I have heard enough! Artan! You are disqualified!

»I declare Kern winner of the Challenge. He is the new First Apprentice.«

»HA! Sucks to you, you little stinker!« grinned Kern, pointing a finger at Artan. »I'm the First Apprentice!!«

»And your first task is to clean all the blackboards,« Lorgo went on calmly. Kern's jaw dropped.

»What? But ... I'm the First Apprentice?!« howled Kern. »I don't do slave work!«

»The most important lesson a First Apprentice must learn is humility. It may take some time where you're concerned, Kern ...«

Artan couldn't help enjoying Kern's dismay, but it didn't change the fact that he had been disqualified himself.

He stood staring into space, while Lorgo called the houseman to get Kern started on his work. Then the old master came back to Artan.

»Don't look so sad, Artan!«

But sir ... I would have liked to be First Apprentice. Even if it meant having to clean the blackboards all year round!

Reading-Master Lorgo started to laugh quietly to himself. »Yes, you would probably have been the best First Apprentice the Academy has ever had,« he said.

But you are destined for another task!

Artan looked up at Lorgo in consternation. The Reading Master smiled and pointed to Artan's arm. The taynikma glinted in the light from the oil lamp.

»What is that task, sir?« asked Artan.

»Only your destiny can tell you that,« said Lorgo in a serious tone. »Your time as apprentice here at the Academy is ended now.«

»Ended? But ...«

»You have passed your final test, Artan,« said Reading-Master Lorgo, laying a hand on his shoulder. »From now on you must follow your own destiny.«

Artan had a queer feeling in his stomach as he stepped out through the Academy's main gate. A bit sad, but also eager to see where the road would take him. Luckily, he wouldn't have to walk it alone.

Now on to
Book 5: **The
Secret Arena**

Reader's Pages

Welcome to your own Taynikma pages! This is where we bring drawings and greetings from other Taynikma readers.

Send in your drawings or write to us with your questions. If we publish your contribution we will send the book to you free of charge!

Reader Drawings

Eek Mania! Check out these drawings of the eek, the monster facing Koto in Taynikma Book 2: **"The Rats"**. These drawings come from Ruby Hillman, Clay Hillman and Yacub Jamhin.

The Knomes appeared in Taynikma Book 1: **"Master Thief"**. Here they are, drawn by Ruby and Clay Hillman

Reader Question
"Hey Taynikma! Cool books. I've just read the first two. Are there any more?"

Answer

Yes, you have a lot more Taynikma action to look forward to! Ask your local bookseller or go online to buy the books. You can also buy directly from www.taynikma.co.uk

Send your drawings and greetings to:

**Taynikma
PO Box 6268
London W1A 2HE**
mail@taynikma.co.uk

Facial expressions

Facial expressions are what give your characters life.
If they don't reflect some sort of feeling the story soon
becomes boring. Imagine what it would be like if Koto
had the same expression on his face in every single
picture. No fun!

So practice drawing happy, mad, surprised or shocked
faces, if you want to tell stories that are fun for others
to read.

A good way to practice is to look in the mirror and make a lot of faces. Afterwards you can try drawing these in a very simplified way: just a round face with eyes, nose and mouth.

If that works out, you can draw the same expression, but with more details in the face.

Very happy   Suspicious   Furious

Just remember – the more you exaggerate the expression, the more fun it is for the reader.

Sketching

Making a series like Taynikma, we have to invent a lot of weird creatures. In order to make them as different from each other as we can we have to make a lot of sketches and keep trying to find different shapes and faces.

In Book 2, **The Rats**, we had to figure out how Mamma would look. This is what we knew about her:
She can spit acid and has massive, strong arms.
She uses sonar echo, like bats do, to locate her prey.
She moves as easily in water as on land.
She is carnivorous.

Before we found a shape that both Merlin and I were satisfied with, I had made more than 10 sketches. Here are some of them:

In this version I tried a combination of a crocodile and a lizard.

Maybe she should have big ears and small eyes, to show that she finds her prey by hearing, not by sight.

Here we have her walking on her hind legs but she still has webbed fingers.

And here is the version we chose. With a massive jaw that can really crunch up her victims.

TAYNIKMA is a series of ten books!

Follow the
adventures
of Koto
here:

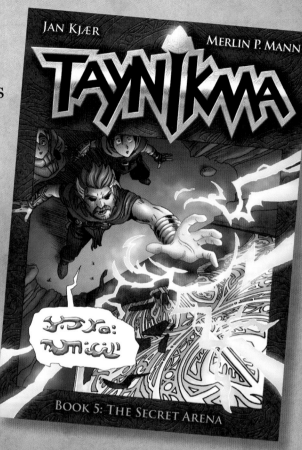

Book 5 will be out soon
- ask at your local book store or shop online

Check for news and updates on our website
www.taynikma.co.uk